Me
(and Charlie)

Me

Charlie

A Life in Bits and Pieces

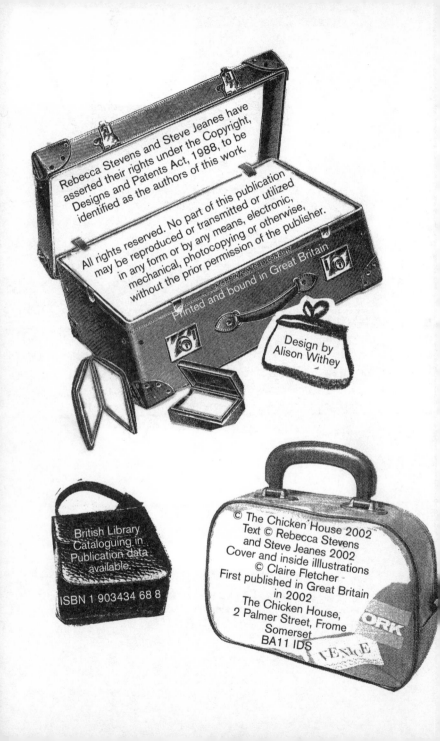

Printed and bound in Great Britain

Design by Alison Withey

British Library Cataloguing in Publication data available.

ISBN 1 903434 68 8

© The Chicken House 2002
Text © Rebecca Stevens and Steve Jeanes 2002
Cover and inside illlustrations © Claire Fletcher
First published in Great Britain in 2002
The Chicken House,
2 Palmer Street, Frome
Somerset
BA11 IDS

Me
(and Charlie)

A Life in Bits and Pieces

Janet Fish and Charlie Wells
Typed by Rebecca Stevens and Steve Jeanes

THANKS TO:

Our mums and dads and sisters cos without them we wouldn't have had much to write about.

To Rebecca Stevens and Steve Jeanes, who typed it for us. They're a couple of oldies who live downstairs. They don't get out much, but their typing's OK, so we let them do this. And we let them be in the book.

To my art teacher, Claire Fletcher, who's forgiven me for the school hall incident, and says that I show promise but need more application. (I think this means I have to use tons of paint.)

To Prince William, because he's GORGEOUS!

This is our first book, but now we've started, I bet we do loads!

Janet.

Janet Fish (Author and Artist) and Him (Charlie Wells – did a few bits and pieces)

(Typed this bit myself – good, eh?)

Sorry about the lip-blots and ink splodges

Chapter One

A major change in your life will bring uncertainty

The first thing you need to know is that I'm not ordinary. And my name's not Janet. My real name's Carmen.

Carmen Amaretto del Fuego Delafonte Passionflower Poisson

But my mum calls me Janet. My mum's all right, in fact she's really nice, but she is quite ordinary and she likes everything else to be ordinary too. In fact, my mum's whole life is one big effort to make things as ordinary as possible. She wants us to live in an ordinary house in an ordinary town and have an ordinary job and go to an ordinary school and have ordinary friends. But I'm not like that. My name's not Janet and I'm not ordinary. I'm extraordinary.

Well.

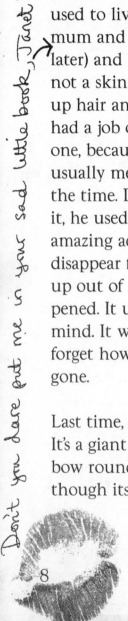

Mum wanting everything to be ordinary was the reason we had to move house. We used to live with my dad, see (that's me, my mum and my sister Dee. More about HER later) and he's like me. Extraordinary, I mean, not a skinny twelve-year-old girl with sticky-up hair and a brace on her teeth. He's never had a job or anything, my dad, not a proper one, because jobs are often quite boring and usually mean you have to stay in one place all the time. Dad didn't want that, couldn't hack it, he used to say. He was always off on some amazing adventure – sometimes he used to disappear for weeks at a time and then turn up out of the blue as if nothing had happened. It used to drive Mum mad, but I didn't mind. It was always so great to see him that I'd forget how much I'd missed him when he was gone.

Last time, he even brought me back a present. It's a giant yellow teddy bear with a pink satin bow round its neck. I really really like it, even though its eyes are a bit stary.

Anyway, eventually Mum got fed up. She told Dad we didn't want him to come back any more (WE didn't – ha!) and he could just take his dirty underpants and his collection of 1970's soul albums and stay on the road forever for all she cared. Dad didn't take any notice, of course, he carried on popping up from time to time just like he always did. He's like that, my dad, nobody can tell him what to do. Well, this made Mum even more mad, of course, and the next thing was, she announced we were moving. Moving! We were going to go some-where Dad couldn't find us so he wouldn't keep turning up and disrupting our lives. That's what she said. And when I said he didn't disrupt MY life, in fact I LIKED it when he turned up out of the blue because he was my dad and I loved him, she didn't say anything at all. Just sort of bit her lip and looked away, with her eyes all stary like my teddy's.

Anyway, Mum got her way. We moved. And so here we are in a new flat in a new part of town where my dad won't be able to come and find us and disrupt our lives.

And my friends won't be able to come and see me either. Not that they'd want to of course. The area we moved to is DEAD boring – full of the kind of people whose idea of a good night out is to stay at home watching telly (i.e. ORDINARY people). Thank goodness I can still e-mail Tiffani. She's my best friend and she's completely and utterly FAB. She lives in this ginormous house in the country with her mum and dad and her big brother (he's a tennis champion called Wills and he's really really good-looking. Tiffani reckons he FANCIES me!) and we're going to be best friends for ever and ever and ever. Even though I've moved miles and miles away.

I suppose the new flat's not TOO bad. I've got my own room (at the old house I had to share with Dee) and Mum says I can decorate it myself so long as we don't have a repeat of the incident with the glue gun and the chicken

In your dreams, Janet! Dee

feathers. I'm really good at that sort of thing (decorating, I mean. I'm probably going to be an interior designer when I leave school) and I know exactly how I want it. It's going to be completely blue, because that's my favourite colour. Not pale blue like babies' cardigans, or navy blue like school uniform, but ROYAL blue. The colour of the sky in the evening after a really sunny day, when the sun's gone down but it's not completely dark yet, you know? The ceiling's going to be covered with stars that really twinkle in the dark, and there'll be a round white light hanging down like the moon, and the walls will be draped with blue velvet curtains. And I'm not going to sleep on a bed, that'd be way too ordinary. I'm going to recline on a pile of silken cushions like a film star out of Mum's magazine.

Because I'm not ordinary. I'm extraordinary. And my name's not Janet.

Goodnight.

This is Charlie ↓

Deirdre incinerated a sausage when she got in from work
last night, which is why I started my day scraping the
black bits out of the bottom of the frying pan. Deirdre's
my mum. She thinks she's still a teenager, even though
she's well ancient. She's thirty-two and she's got a
pierced nose and purple hair! How sad is that?

I'm Charlie. I AM a teenager. I'm twelve years three-and-
a-half months, anyway, and that counts. Mind you, I might
as well be five the amount of time I spend with my kid
sister Geri. She's my half-sister really (half sister, half
psycho killer zombie robot, that is) and I have to look
after her while Deirdre's at work in the evenings. She's a
real pain. I read in a magazine that a bunch of mad
blokes once tried to invent a 'perpetual motion' machine
– something that once you started it, never stopped. Well,
if they'd asked me, I could have told them not to bother. I
live with one, and it's no fun. If there's a toy to fall over,
she'll fall over it. If there's a plate to break, she'll break it.
If there's a bit of old fish-finger under the kitchen table
she'll find it and stick it in her mouth. How she's survived
up till now, I'll never know.

A lot of the boys at school have started going on about
girls and getting girlfriends. They need their heads seeing
to. Let them try living in my flat. What with Purple Hair
Woman in one room and the Human Tornado in the other,
I've already got two too many women in my life, thank you
very much. Why would I want another one?

12

As I said, the day started as usual with Deirdre flapping around upstairs, Geri beginning her routine destruction of the living room, and me in the kitchen, trying to clean out the frying pan. I thought things couldn't get any worse. I was well wrong.

To: Tiffani
From: Janet
Subject: NEW SCHOOL

My new school's HUGE. It's got a theatre and a swimming pool and a proper drama studio and three art rooms and miles and miles of long, gleaming white corridors that go on for ever and ever and the hall's so big that when you stand in the middle you can hardly see the edges. It's LOADS bigger than the old place. I think I'm really going to love it.

The only thing wrong is that you're not there. I'm sure I'll make loads of new friends, but nobody could ever take your place, Tiff, because you're my BEST friend.

Love

Your best friend
Carmen Amaretto del Fuego Delafonte
Passionflower Poisson x

There IS something wrong with my new
school actually, but I wasn't going to tell Tiff.
It's a BOY. He's in my class and his name's
Charles. Charles!

14

Like Prince Charles (ha!). Which is a pretty good name for him actually because he's just about as boring and ordinary as the real Prince Charles. If he was called WILLIAM it'd be a different matter, of course. I mean, William might be a pretty ordinary name but nobody could call Prince William ordinary, could they? Whereas his poor old dad . . . well, if you had a face like his would YOU go swanning round the world shaking hands with famous people and getting yourself on telly all the time? No. You'd stay at home with a sack over your head for the Good of the Nation and leave all the swanning around shaking hands bit to your son. He'd be so much better at it and he wouldn't make everyone feel sick every time they saw him on the news. Don't get me wrong, I'm a one hundred per cent supporter of the Royal Family. I just think they should make Prince William king straight away and make all the others go and live on a council estate somewhere horrible. That'd shut them up.

Anyway.

Charlie

This boy Charles isn't a prince and he's not good-looking, which along with everything else must make him about the most super-ordinary person ever (which ought to make him extraordinary, I know, but some- how doesn't) and I ended up having to be partners with him...

What happened was this.

I got to school a bit late because Mum didn't realise how long it would take to get there (or that most people don't let their mums take them to school when they're older than about six-and-a-half) and when I eventually found my classroom everybody stopped what they were doing and stared at me. One girl in par- ticular was REALLY staring. She was dead pretty and nice-looking (her name's Daisy) and I reckon she was probably thinking that I might be good to have for a new best friend because while she was looking at me she whis- pered something to the girl sitting next to her and they both laughed in a really friendly way.

Anyway. After we'd done a bit of maths, Mr Walker (he's my form teacher and he's got REALLY sad hair) said we had to get into pairs for this Art Project thing. I hoped he'd put me with Daisy, but no such luck. Guess who he put me with? That's right. Old Prince Charlie (he was the only other one who didn't have a partner – wonder why, huh?).

So. This was what we had to do for the Art Project:

ART PROJECT

Design a mural to decorate either:

1. The wall at the end of the big playground.

OR

2. The music room.

OR

3. The school hall.

Well, it had to be the hall, didn't it, because it was just so BIG.

What we had to do was go round the school (with our partners), look at the walls, think up some ideas, do sketches, etc. Then we were to go back to the classroom, do our design and write up how we planned to 'execute' it. Later on, there'd be an exhibition of all the designs and everyone in the school would vote for the one they liked best and if it was good enough it would actually be carried out!

Fun, eh?

Well, it should've been. I had this absolutely brilliant idea, you see. Nobody else wanted to do the hall – they all chose the playground because it meant they could hang around outside and chat. But not me. I wanted the hall. The real beauty of my idea was that it could be done STRAIGHT AWAY – without having to bother with all the sketching and designing and stuff.

And all it needed was a big pot of paint (blue, of course), the ropes hanging from the walls (the hall's used as a gym as well, you see) and ME. But old Prince Charles wouldn't go for it. In fact,

he said that if I insisted on doing it, he was going
to tell Mr Walker! Well, I had no alternative, did
I? I had to lock him in the games cupboard.

She thought I was going to tell Walker! No way! I'm not a
sneak. I just knew that I had to stop her or there'd be big
trouble. But when I tried to reason with her she got this
really weird look in her eye and started humming loudly
and out of tune, so she couldn't hear what I was saying.
Next thing I know I'm on my back in the games cupboard
on a pile of gym mats with the door slammed shut.
Perfect.

With him out of the way, I set about gathering
together my equipment. I went to the art room
(I knew where it was because I'd passed the door
when I arrived) and told the teacher that Mr
Walker had asked me to get a big pot of blue
paint and one of those tray things you use with
a roller. She looked a bit surprised, but gave
them to me anyway – people always do if you
ask them in a confident enough voice, I find.

When I got back to the hall, the noises from
the games cupboard had stopped (I think
Charles quite liked it in there, actually), so I
could settle down to work in peace.

Now. I hope you don't shock easily because what I planned to do was a bit – well, a bit UNUSUAL I suppose. A bit AVANT GARDE as we say in the art biz. Most great artists are ahead of their time, you see, and it takes time for ordinary people to get used to their ideas.

What I was going to do was use the gym ropes to create a beautiful design of giant blue butterflies, fluttering over the walls. And how was I going to do it? I was going to use MY OWN BODY. Like this . . .

BOTTOMFLIES!

..... Trouble is, I never got to do it.

I'd poured the paint into the tray, given it a stir and was just about to strip for action when Mr Walker walked in.

Well that was it, wasn't it. Prince Charles was let out of the cupboard, there was a phone call to my mum and I was sent home for the rest of day to 'think about what I'd done'.

My first day at my new school. Wasted.

But there's always tomorrow.

I can't wait...

Chapter Two

New friends are not always what they seem

Well.

You'll never guess what happened this morning. I'd just got up for school, yeah, and was rummaging around in the kitchen for something to eat (Mum says her first priority is to find a job so we haven't had time to do a big shop yet) when the doorbell rang. Nobody else seemed about to open it (Mum being in her bedroom getting dressed and Dee in the bathroom applying her sixtyninth layer of lip gloss), so I did.

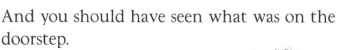

And you should have seen what was on the doorstep.

It was this really weird-looking woman with purple hair and a stud in her nose (Dee wants to get her nose pierced, but I think it's gross. I mean, what happens when you've got a cold? All the snot would come squirting out through the hole when you sneeze). Anyway, soon as I opened the door this woman shot inside, headed straight for the kitchen and started blethering on about how she lived next door and it was so great that me and her son had made friends because he was such a loner and had to spend all his time looking after his little sister and how this made her feel really guilty but she had no choice, etc etc etc. And all I could think was, who was this mad woman, what the heck was she on about and when was she going to clear off so I could get on with my breakfast?

24

And then it dawned on me.

Charles.

She was **Prince Charles's mum!**

Well, the thought of him having a mum like this (it's hard to imagine him having ANY mum, let alone one with purple hair and a stud through her nose who can't stop talking) made me want to laugh so much that when she suggested him and me walk to school together I didn't object. I was quite pleased, actually. I get really bored walking on my own and I could have a bit of fun winding him up about having a mother with purple hair.

So that's what happened. My mum was pleased because I had someone responsible-looking to go to school with and his mum was pleased because she thought her little boy had got himself a friend at last (as if!). We left them alone together in the kitchen drinking tea and yabbering on about what a struggle it is bringing up kids on your own, and set off to school.

And it wasn't too bad actually. The walk, I mean. Well, Prince Charles was still really really boring, of course, but knowing he's got a mum like that made him seem a bit less really really boring, if you see what I mean. That doesn't mean him and me are going to be friends, mind you. No way. Having boys as friends is something you might do when you're, like, eight or nine or something, but I am so past that now.

I'm twelve.

And I'm going to be friends with Daisy.

Did you ever have one of those spots in a really embarrassing place, like the end of your nose, that, no matter how much you squeeze it, it just won't go away. It keeps coming back bigger and redder and even more stupid looking, like it's saying, 'Look at me! Look at me!'? Well, I've got one of those – it's called JANET!

After yesterday's disaster, I swore I'd avoid her like supermarket trainers, but she's only moved in next door, hasn't she, and now Deirdre's making me walk to school with her as well. She thinks we're going to be friends! Deirdre's got this thing about me not having any friends, which is rubbish. I've got loads. I just don't bring them home. I'd like to keep them.

So there we are, the only time of day I get to myself, and I've got to put up with this maniac running around, sticking her nose in all the shops and saying hello to total strangers and talking non-stop. Did I say talking? She was more like an explosion in a words factory. Half the time she didn't even make sense. Gibbering away in my ear, jumping from one subject to another without taking any notice of what I had to say, which wasn't a lot, admittedly. I didn't have much chance, even when she made some rude comment about Deirdre's hair. She didn't even seem to notice me pulling my jacket further and further up round my ears so nobody I knew would recognise me. I mean, you hang out with loonies, people start thinking you're one too.

It's a fair walk to school, unfortunately, so by the time we got there, I knew everything I would ever want to know about Janet Fish. And quite a few things I wouldn't. Like how she was going to be a famous artist, or maybe an actress or maybe something called a performance artist which was sort of the two mixed up. Or maybe even drive a really huge bulldozer and use it to make fantastic sculptures out of earth.

I told her she'd be able to start her career sooner than she thought – she'd be kicked out of school quick enough if she insisted on decorating it with blue bum-prints. When I said that, she started doing this impression of a bulldozer chugging up and down the street, banging into lampposts and pillar boxes and bushes and struggling to push them over. It was actually quite funny, but I wasn't going to laugh, it might have made her start thinking we were friends or something. Then she turned the corner, and bulldozed her way right into this great ferocious looking Rottweiler. I knew that it belonged to Mrs Goldstein from the chip shop and wouldn't hurt a fly, but the look on her face. . .! I couldn't help it, I laughed so much, I almost parked my breakfast.

When Mushy (the dog) gave her a great slobbery lick-ing, she realised what a big softy he was, and looked like someone does when they've been trying to push a door open for ages and you point out the sign saying 'pull'. For a moment, I almost liked her. Almost. Then she started prattling on and on and on again, until I thought my ears were going to drop off.

By the time we walked into the playground, it seemed like I'd been listening to her voice ringing around in my head for most of my life.

Morning school was OK. We had very fun history with gorgeous Mr Green (did you know that the Victorians used to let really young girls work as COAL MINERS? How cool is that?!) and then very not fun geography with a woman with big hairy warts all over her face. If I was her I'd have them surgically removed, but maybe that's just me. I don't care as much about my appearance as someone like Dee (she once stayed in bed for a week because she thought her knees were too low down), but I do have some standards. Like I wouldn't want to make people feel physically sick because my face was all covered in big hairy growths, you know? Especially if I was trying to teach them geography.

cool!

You're dead, Janet, DEAD! Dee xx

Anyway.

At lunchtime something horrible happened.
I'd been trying to catch Daisy's eye all morning.
I just knew she wanted to be friends
but every time I looked over she
seemed to be whispering and laughing with the girl sitting next to her
(she's called China and she wears the
sort of shoes my mum would say are
REALLY INAPPROPRIATE for
school). So I was looking forward to
lunchtime break when we'd have a
chance to get to know each other
properly.

Well. I wandered into the hall after lunch (it
was raining so we couldn't go outside, worse
luck) and came across Daisy and some other
girls hanging out by the girls' toilets. They
were practising this dance routine they'd
copied from some group on TV. Apparently
there's this Stars for a Night thing happening
at school next week and Daisy was planning
to perform it then but without her mates.
Well, I reckoned their dance routine was

30

completely and utterly rubbish. They looked like three old grannies trying to scrape something stinky off their shoes, so I suggested a few ways of livening it up a bit.

groovy

groovy

groovy

Well.

I thought they'd be really glad of the help but instead of being grateful they got all huffy and horrible and Daisy said why would they need help from a saddo loser like me who obviously didn't know the first thing about pop music?

And they all laughed.

Well, you can imagine
how that made me feel.

It made me MAD.

Because, apart from
anything else, it is just
so rubbish. I know LOADS about pop
music, probably more than any other twelve-
year-old girl in the entire history of the world.

How come?

Because of my dad, that's how come.

He's an international rock star, you see, who's
had loads and loads of really successful records
and is really mega rich and if you've never
heard of him that's because it's you who's the
saddo loser, not me!

That's what I told Daisy anyway.

And it's true. My dad IS a musician (that's why

he has to go away so
much. He's On Tour)
and he IS really good.
It's just that he's not
COMPLETELY rich
and famous
because he's not
actually made any
records. Yet. He will
soon, of course. It's only
a matter of time before
some record company
spots how good he is and

signs him up and gives him loads of money
and he'll buy a ginormous house in the country
like Tiffani's where we'll all live happily ever
after for ever and ever amen. After all, he's
only forty-two and loads of rock stars don't
make it big until they're way older than that.

But whenever he makes it big won't be soon
enough for me. Not now. Because after I said
all that stuff to Daisy I went and did something REALLY stupid.

I said I could prove it.

HELP!

Nobody believed me, you see. In fact Daisy said she reckoned I didn't have a dad at all, let alone one who was a big famous rock star! And when I said I did, he just had to be away from home a lot, that's all, she said, yes well, THAT was probably because he couldn't stand the sight of ME. And they all laughed again. So I said I'd prove it. I said that by the day of their stupid Stars for a Night thing I'd prove that I DO have a dad and that he IS a really brilliant musician and that he DOES love me VERY VERY much.

That shut them up.

I couldn't even get away from Janet at lunchtime! Crash, bang, wallop, there she was, slapping her tray down and scattering peas everywhere, and then off she went again. Rabbit, rabbit, rabbit. Only this time, it was just the one subject. Daisy Micklepage and how wonderful she was. That's a laugh!

Daisy Micklepage is a grade one pustule. You heard it here first. If her nose was any further in the air, they'd have to put a warning light on it. The only reason

34

anyone's friends with her is because she's tall and blonde and loud, and there's a swimming pool at her parents' house where her 'special' people are invited in summer, to swim and have all-day parties. Her 'special' people don't include what she calls the 'Single Parent Saddos' of course.

But nothing I could say would persuade motormouth Janet otherwise, not that I managed to get a word in, as usual. They were going to be very best friends, and that was that.

So you can imagine what a hoot it was when, after lunch, I spotted the pair of them getting all hot and bothered in the hall. I could tell something was up because Janet was doing that humming thing just like she did before she shut me in the gym cupboard. And I was right. I thought there might be a fight for a moment, which would have been great, cos I reckon Janet could have taken stuck-up Daisy in three. Daisy's tall, but Janet's wiry. But when Janet finished her rant she just turned round and stomped off. Shame. Maybe next time.

I felt really good after I'd told Daisy and her cronies about my dad.

I don't feel good any more though.

Because the show's on Monday.

Which means I've got the weekend to prove that my dad's an international rock star.

Don't worry. I'll think of something.

I just don't know what it is.

Yet.

I'll think of something.

Chapter Three

An unexpected invitation will bring you joy

To: Tiffani
From: Janet
Subject: New School #2

You know how I said my new school was great?

I was wrong.

My new school's horrible. I hate everything about it. I hate the teachers, I hate the kids, I hate the lessons. But most of all I hate this GIRL called DAISY MICKLEPAGE.

I hate her so much that I might just have to kill her. I might just have to creep into her room in the dead of night with a great big carving knife and chop her up into little tiny chunks and feed her to that big dog we saw on the way to

And that was as far as I got. Because while I was writing, another e-mail arrived (the computer's in my room at the new flat because

Mum reckons I use it the most, which is true) and I just had to check it out. Now, we don't get many e-mails in our house because we've only just gone online and hardly anyone knows our e-mail address (mine is: janet@itagain.com. Pretty cool eh?) so it could've been one of two things:

1. Someone trying to make us join some stupid money scheme that's supposed to make us all into millionaires. . .

OR

2. My dad.

dad

Guess which it was?

That's right. This is what he said:

To: Janet
From: Wizzo
Subject: life

hey gorgeous howzabout paying yr poor old pa a
visit? I've got this great gig manana (ie saturday)
at an old pal's wedding do (remember me old mate
scuz? the one with the glass eye and the mad
hair? well he's only gone and got himself a woman
hasn't he! hey if he can do it there's hope for us
all!!!!) anyway it's going to be completely and
utterly fabuloso and guess what scuz says i can
invite a couple of guests of my own! so i thought
i'd see if that madonna bird fancied tagging along
ha ha just joking i thought i'd invite u! what d'ya
reckon? (but ask la mama first – we don't want to
go upsetting her again do we? not after what happened last time)

hasta la vista baby and bring a pal

love
yr poor old dad
sad, bad wizzo x :)

ps address of gig, etc attached. do come, honey-
bunch, i miss u heaps. And i've got a surprise for
u. which I THINK u might like.......

Love love love ....

Well.

That made me feel so much
better I never finished my
e-mail to Tiffani (I WAS going to
ask her if I could go and stay with her in her
ginormous house for a few weeks until Daisy
had forgotten about my dad and everything,
but suddenly that didn't seem important any
more).

Because I had a brilliant
idea.

If I went to see my
dad at this wedding
'thing
then I
could ask
him to come
along to Stars for a Night
next week. I might even be able to persuade him to PLAY.

And?

Soooo
happy

Brilliant !

41

Get real Janet! He's like from the ark! He even plays his own guitar! Dees

And THAT would prove to everyone that I DID have a dad and that he WAS a brilliant musician and that he DID love me VERY VERY much. And Daisy would look a right idiot and feel as sick as a pig and I would be the most popular girl in the class!

Problem solved!

Apart from that, of course, it would be just so fantastic to see my dad again that I felt like I was going to explode in a cloud of stars all over my new bedroom (and what about the Surprise? What could that be? I couldn't wait!).

So I went through to the kitchen to ask Mum if I could go.

And guess what?

She said no.

42

Football practice was great. One goal, one assist. One red card. What a total wazzock. Who brings out red cards in a practice? Arfy Jones, that's who. Some games teacher. I bet he's never played anything in his life. Ten minutes running around and he's purple. I bet he red-carded me just to get a breather. It was only a little tap, anyway. There was hardly any blood.

Whatever, I made an impression. I reckoned I was that far away from making the team. Meanwhile, I had this plan. Though I hadn't been picked, I was going down to watch the team play on Saturday, and I was taking my kit. The game was against Meltham HIgh, the dirtiest team in the league. It would only take a couple of stretchering-offs and they'd be looking around for a replacement. Someone who doesn't mind a bit of physical contact. . .

I came home whistling happily to myself. In the kitchen, Deirdre was entertaining her weird old hippy friend Gandolfo. Or is its Golem? Or Gadalfi? Something stupid like that. Gandolfo makes Deirdre look like a bank manager. I'm sure he's responsible for a lot of the stories you hear about people seeing aliens from outer space. If you didn't know, you'd swear he wasn't human. I won't go into details, it would take too long. I'll just say he makes all his own clothes, mostly out of things people wouldn't dream of wearing, like cushion covers or carpet, he has the kind of hair that you expect a flock of crows to come screeching out of at any moment, and he likes to paint his face. All over. In metallic paint.

Weirdo, or what? But what he does to himself could never match what he's been given at birth. Gandolfo has far and away the biggest nose that's ever been seen on the planet, or whichever planet he comes from. It's like the rudder on an ocean liner. If it was windy, he couldn't turn his head sideways, because the wind would just keep blowing it back. It's COLOSSAL.

At one time, I had the horrible feeling that Gandolfo might be my dad, but a look in the bathroom mirror soon cured me of that. My nose is just fine.

I've heard rumours that he's rolling in it, but there's no sign of that. Gandolfo lives in some filthy old bus that he drives around from one hippy festival to another. No sensible person would do that if they had money. Still, who can tell. Gandolfo isn't what you'd call sensible. Anyway, him and Deirdre have always been the best of mates and whenever he's around they spend hours and hours and hours just sitting around in the kitchen drinking endless cups of tea and cackling hysterically. So I said hello, and went off to clean my boots in the bathroom, and think about my tactics for the match.

Then Deirdre called through to tell me the bad news about Saturday. . .

Can you believe it?

Mum said I couldn't go anywhere tomorrow because she'd arranged for me to go round and 'play' with Charlie (PLAY!!!! I haven't been round to PLAY with anybody since I was about six-and-a-half). Apparently she'd got some last minute job interview and there was no way she was going to leave me alone in the flat, not after what happened last time (which was nothing really. I found this tin of paint in the cupboard under the stairs

Me aged 6½.

45

at our old house and decided to do a bit of decorating, that's all. I thought I did a really good job, but when Mum came back she just screamed. Apparently you're not supposed to paint the inside of baths. Especially not with red paint. Mum said it looked like I'd slaughtered a pig). Anyway, DEE wasn't available to babysit (BABYSIT! I'm TWELVE) because she'd already arranged to go off and spend the day with her friends hanging round the lip-gloss counter in Boots, surprise surprise, and there was NO WAY Mum was going to allow me to go gallivanting halfway across town to see Dad on my own. No way.

So that was that.

Well, I tried to reason with her, of course. But she wasn't about to budge. She said she'd already spoken to Charlie's mum (her name's DEIRDRE! How mad is that? WEIRDRE, more

Dee? Janet, hanging round the lip gloss counter in Boots, with reality at all? Are you in touch with reality at all? There is no lip gloss counter in Boots,

like!) and arranged for me to spend the WHOLE DAY with them. And when I said you must be kidding I'd rather DIE than spend a whole day with him and his weirdo mother, she said she was sick of me being difficult and that it would be nice if I gave her some support over this for a change because if she didn't get a job soon we wouldn't be able to pay the rent and we'd be thrown out of our flat and have to live in a cardboard box under the railway bridge! So I said that living in a cardboard box under the railway bridge sounded a whole lot more fun than living in a horrible flat with a stupid sister whose only interest in life was lip-gloss and a boring bossy mother who won't let me do anything, even go and see my own dad!

Small but
soooooo cosy.

47

And she didn't say anything to that.

She just did the stary thing with her eyes and looked out of the window.

I hate it when she does that. It makes me feel all bad and empty inside like there's no point in anything and everything's awful. And I get this horrible burny feeling behind my eyes as if my brain's trying to cry but my eyes can't.

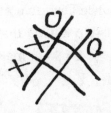

So I stopped arguing and went to bed.

But when Mum and I had made up and she'd kissed me goodnight and shut the door I suddenly remembered something.

I hadn't replied to my dad's e-mail.

Well, I had to do THAT, didn't I? I didn't want him to think I didn't care. . .

I was really fed up. Sometimes Deirdre doesn't seem to care about anything I want, so, when Gandolfo'd gone, I tried to put my case. I told her I wasn't going to hang around with Janet on Saturday, and she told me I was. So I told her I wasn't, and she told me . . . well, you know how it goes, but then she just seemed to lose interest. I couldn't work out what was the matter. She just kept staring into space, every now and again saying 'eh?' and then still not listening. In the end, I had to stand on the table right in front of her to get her attention. When she finally shook herself out of her funk, it turned out she was upset about Gandolfo. He was off for a year to live with some tribe in the Amazon jungle. And the best of luck to him. Great fun if you like eating bugs. Geri would love it. Anyway, Deirdre had a big soft spot for the old weirdo, and she was really going to miss him. She was even snuffling a bit. I couldn't go on arguing when she was feeling that way. Eventually, she gave a great long sigh, then, looking up at the kitchen clock went into her usual 'late for work' panic. She threw her coat on, let Mrs Abercrombie across the hall know she was off (Mrs Abercrombie keeps an eye on us while Deirdre's at work), and ran for the bus. I didn't like to tell her that she looked like a startled panda where all her make-up had run. I expect she'll find out when she gets there. She might even like it that way.

It didn't take me long to forget about Saturday. Geri was having one of her 'days'. Something to do with the full moon, I reckon. I saw this programme on the telly all about how the moon affects us, even though we don't notice it most of the time. You know, like werewolves and that, only not quite as hairy. Round comes the full moon and we practically have to tie Geri down. It was full moon that weekend. She started off by getting one foot trapped down the back of the settee while she was bouncing up and down on it, then screaming her head off until I managed to free it. After that, I thought she'd quietened down, sitting, silently watching TV eating a bag of chocolate buttons. It took me a minute to realise that they weren't. Chocolates I mean. They were real ones. I got them away from her, but not before she'd eaten enough to make her rattle.

I was keeping a very close eye on her after that, but she just started crawling in circles around the settee. She's been walking for years, but she still likes to crawl now and again. Probably the full moon wolf in her. Anyway, that seemed reasonably harmless, but the moment I looked away, she speeded up like a mad thing, put her hand on a cheese sandwich she'd left lying about on the floor, and skidded so that her head jammed sideways under the sideboard.

Ten minutes of crying (her) and tugging (me), and she was finally free, and we were both exhausted. Only damage, two very red ears. I carried her off to bed and read her a story, but she was fast asleep before I'd hardly begun. I grabbed a drink from the fridge and slumped back on the settee to think about my day.

And the next one.

A whole day with Janet. Oh, joy.

To: Tiffani
From: Janet
Subject: My Dad!

Great news! My dad's playing at this wedding tomorrow and he's invited me along! Mum says I've got to go round and spend the day with this boring boy who lives next door, but guess what?

That's right. You can read me like a book, Tiff... I've got other plans.

Chapter Four

Beware of small creatures with sharp teeth: they bite!

I've changed my mind about how I'm going to decorate my bedroom. It's not going to be blue anymore. It's going to be purple. Purple walls, purple floor, purple curtains. Purple ceiling. And instead of the big pile of cushions to sleep on it's going to have a huge great mattress on the floor covered with an amazing Indian bedspread all embroidered with elephants and stuff and with tiny little mirrors sewn all over it that sparkle in the light. And hanging down from the ceiling there's going to be a mirror ball (like in a disco) so that when you draw the curtains in the morning and the sun comes in, the room looks like it's full of a million dancing snowflakes made of light. . .

my bedroom

It'll be like living inside one of those glass snowstorm things (except not wet, obviously).

Where we live has always been quite ordinary. But Charlie's flat. . .

Well, you'd just have to see it, that's all.

It's – amazing.

Particularly his mum's bedroom (which is what I've based my ideas on). She doesn't bother with shelves or cupboards or anything like that. All her clothes and jewellery and stuff are draped over this old dummy out of a shop window (I don't know HOW she got hold of it) and everything else is just dumped in a heap in the corner.

Even Charlie's room is quite cool (though so tidy it's scary). He's got the computer in there (must get his address so I can send him an e-mail) and the walls are painted metallic silver. And he hasn't got any stupid posters or anything (not like Dee – her old room was covered with pictures of this grinning boy singer with

huge teeth and a
shiny chest. How sad is
that?) – he's just got one
of those clocks that project
the time onto the wall in
light and a desk with a big
lighty-up globe on it and –

And I'm beginning to
think I might have been
wrong about him.

Well, not that wrong.
He's obviously QUITE
boring.

But maybe he's not so VERY boring as I
thought. I may even begin to like him.

A bit.

I can tell Janet doesn't like me, though she liked my
room, but why should I give a stuff? I don't really care
if she does or not. She's the most self-obsessed person I've ever met – always talking about herself and
never taking any notice of what I say.

54

Typical.

I'M the one who gets shoved in a cupboard. I'M the one who has to walk her to school. AND I'M THE ONE WHO MISSES WHAT COULD WELL BE THE MOST IMPORTANT FOOTBALL MATCH OF MY CAREER SO FAR! Just so she can be entertained. Do I get an apology? You must be joking!

What I get is:

'Oh! Isn't this room gorgeous! Oh! Where did your mum get that dummy? Oh! I'm going to do my room in purple now. With a dummy. Though I bet that can be really spooky. You know, the dummy. I'm not sure if I'd want that standing next to my bed at night. It would be like the Attack of the Mummy. Attack of the Dummy! Ha, ha!

'Oooooooooooo! I know! I could put a light on the top and kind of make it into a bedside lamp. Oo! Oo! Then I could put coloured scarves on it, purple ones, so it made purple light. Or I could put red ones on so it was like a big red brain on a space monster, throb-bing in the dark. Oh, maybe that would be scary too. But it would be really cool! Or maybe forget the dummy. I could be an artist, all dressed in silk pyjamas, purple silk pyjamas, draped over cushions and looking very mysterious. I'm mysterious, aren't I? Very mysterious?'

And on and on. Me, me, me, me, me. The trouble with Janet, (apart from the obvious one – she's Janet) is that she doesn't know anything about the important things in life. She doesn't know anything about football or Playstations or how to get your hair to go in spikes.

Geri seemed to like her though.

The one thing that is seriously NOT cool about Charlie's flat is his SISTER. Well, he SAYS she's his sister but I have my doubts. Sisters have to be human beings, after all (if you're a human being yourself, of course. Obviously if you're an elephant or a bee or a wombat then your sister would be an elephant or a bee or a wombat too). I don't know what she is, but I'm sure she's not human. She's more like some horrible little demon thing (you know those carved stone creatures you get on the outsides of churches? What are they called, gargoyles. She's like one of them. Only not made of stone, worse luck. Or stuck up on top of a church). She's got sticky-out ears and these tiny little dark eyes that look like someone's poked two holes in her face and she's behind it looking out, like some nasty little sharp-toothed wild animal waiting to attack you from behind a hedge. There's one animal in particular that she reminds me of, but I can't remember what it's called.

Anyway.

Charlie says that Geri (that's her name) refuses to do anything normal like wash or wear knickers and that her favourite pastimes are scraping old food off the underside of the kitchen table and eating it and making life miserable for Charlie.

And that's not the worst thing.

She bites.

Geri

As soon as I walked in the door (Mum had gone off for her interview looking all smart and nervous and un-mum-like wearing lip-stick and a worried expression. She looked so much more like a scared little girl than a grown-up mother person that I felt all weird and couldn't look at her when she told me to wish her luck) Geri jumped out from under the table and fastened her teeth on my leg.

She only got a mouthful of jeans, thank good-ness, but it still isn't what you want when you go round to somebody's house. Not the first time anyway. So – after I'd shaken her off – I asked her what the heck she thought she was doing and she said...

'I want to see your bloo-ood......'

... in this really scary voice like something out of a horror film. Charlie says she does it all the time. His mum reckons she'll grow out of it by

the time she starts school but I have my doubts. She doesn't look like she's ever going to grow out of anything. Apparently the nearest primary is a church school as well, so she's going to have to start wearing knickers if she goes there. I can't imagine them letting her in otherwise.

Ok, so this is a 'hamster'

Tasmanian Devil.

of.

That's the animal she reminds me of. They're small but deadly with beady little eyes, razor sharp teeth and the ability to scare off their ↗enemies by making their ears turn red.

Janet, you're making this up.

Just like her.

Of course, Janet didn't realise Geri was just being friendly. She only bites people she likes. She really HURTS the ones she hates. She runs at them with her head down so that she knocks all the air out of them and they collapse on the floor holding their stomach. Then she'll play horsey with them while they lie on the floor moaning. Jumping up and down on them, shouting 'Giddy-up!' That's a big favourite with her. I can prove she bites people she likes. I've got bites all up my legs, and I'm as close to a friend as Geri's got.

Anyway, what with Geri having taken a liking to Miss Motormouth, and Janet hardly noticing my existence, I began to wonder what was the point of me being there at all.

Once I'd given Janet the grand tour (grand! Ha, ha! You could fit our entire flat into a shoe-box), I spotted that she'd lost interest entirely. She was so busy talking about herself that I didn't think she'd notice if I was there or not.

So I started thinking about not.

Deirdre was in the kitchen making a pot of tea. I was on the settee, trying to look fascinated while Janet went on and on about whether her room should have an Eastern theme or whether it should be more nineteenth-century Parisian. I didn't have the faintest idea what she was on about, and I didn't want to ask, even if I'd had the chance to, in case she burbled on for another hour or so. There was rugby on the telly later, and even though I was missing the football, I wasn't going to miss that as well.

It was beginning to seem like Janet would talk straight through the rugby too, but Geri started 'looking' at her, and that's when I got my chance.

I write 'looking' like that because when Geri looks at you, it's not always just looking. Sometimes she does it in a really funny way. It's a bit like a crocodile peering at a deer nervously drinking at the edge of the river. You can almost see in the crocodile's eyes that it's weighing up just how many dinners it'll get from the deer. Geri can 'look' a bit like that.

Anyway, this is exactly what Geri did. At Janet. And Janet shut up! Old Flapping Jaw, silent! Just like that! I made a mental note to take Geri aside and get her to teach me that look. Then Geri started crawling towards Janet, and Janet was up off the settee like a gazelle who's seen the water moving. She said something about helping Deirdre in the kitchen and shot out of there like somebody had lit her blue touchpaper. It was my golden opportunity.

I gave Geri a chocolate biscuit to show her my appreciation, also because it pays to stay on her good side, and dashed off to my room.

I was just shoving my football kit into its bag, and wondering if anybody at all would notice that I wasn't there, when all this shrieking started coming from the living room.

After Charlie had shown me round and I was just beginning to get bored and wonder how I was going to escape and get off to see my dad, it happened. The Tasmanian Devil started making these weird wailing noises and rolling round on the floor, clutching her stomach. I was quite shocked but Deirdre just turned the radio up and carried on drinking her tea, so I realised it was the kind of thing that must happen all the time. Trouble is, it didn't stop. It went on and on and on, getting louder and louder and louder. Eventually the noise level got so bad that even Deirdre couldn't bear it so she turned off the radio and asked the TD (i.e. Tasmanian Devil) what was wrong.

Well.

The TD said that her tummy

really really really really really really really really really really really really really really HURT.

You would've thought that might've got
        Deirdre a bit worried, wouldn't you? If
        she was a normal mother, that is.

        Well, Deirdre's not. A normal
mother, I mean.

If anything it seemed to reassure
her. She just said something like
well, that'd be down to the five Poptarts you
had for breakfast then, chickypoo, and turned
the radio on again.

But it made Charlie go all funny.

He turned OFF the radio and started
blethering on to Deirdre about how he
thought it might be serious. Apparently
he'd found Geri eating a bag of buttons (that's
REAL buttons, not the chocolate kind ha ha)
the night before and she'd swallowed some of
        them before he could get them off her
        and maybe THAT was why
        she had a tummy ache?!!!!!

I didn't take much notice at first. Geri likes a good shriek. If she's in a really good mood, she can shriek long enough and loud enough to make glasses on a shelf shake, or old ladies throw up, so it's nothing new in our house. Deirdre usually just turns the radio up until it stops. Only, this time it didn't stop. Then . . . then I remembered the buttons, and I got a bad feeling.

I really, really wanted to go and play football, but . . .

There was no way round it. I'd have to tell Deirdre about the buttons. I'm sure Geri could swallow half the planet and the only side effect would be a loud burp, but I couldn't take the chance. If something happened to my little sister, I'd never forgive myself. It was confession time.

Well, that did the trick, didn't it? Deirdre went spare, rushed out into the street and flagged down the first car she saw, which screeched to a halt, narrowly avoiding hitting her. Before the driver could ask her what the heck she thought she was up to, she'd climbed in the back with Geri (who by now was wailing like a police siren) and demanded to be taken to

the nearest Accident and Emergency
Department. Well, he could hardly refuse,
could he?

So that was that.

They drove off to the hospital, leaving me and Charlie all on our own in the flat with no-one to make sure we stayed there.

Oh dear. . .

Chapter Five

It is better to remain silent than to hurt a friend

Well, he wouldn't do it, would he?

No matter what I said, Charlie absolutely refused to come with me to see my dad.

I tried everything. I begged, I pleaded, I bullied. I told him that I hadn't seen Dad for months and months and months and that this was probably my last chance – if I didn't see him today I would probably have to wait for YEARS before I got to see him again because he was just about to set off on a major expedition to the North Pole where he was going to study the drinking habits of penguins and he might even die of frostbite and then I'd

NEVER get to see him again and it would be all Charlie's fault.

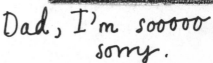

And did that work?

Of course not.

Dad, I'm sooooo sorry.

Charlie just looked at me and said he thought my dad was a famous rock musician, not an explorer, and didn't I know that penguins come from the South Pole, not the North?

Well, that was a bit annoying so I had to think fast. I said, yeah, well, maybe it wasn't penguins after all, but polar bears, but that wasn't important because my dad IS a famous rock musician who just happens to like animals as well and didn't Charlie know that a lot of people nowadays have more than one job because of the economic climate? (I'm not quite sure what that means but think it's something to do with global warming). I don't know if I was on safe ground with the polar bear stuff but it seemed to shut him up. He just made a sort of snorting noise and carried on clearing the table.

(You might be wondering why I didn't just go off to see Dad on my own. Well, I could've done, of course, but I didn't think Deirdre would like it if I left Charlie on his own in the flat. And it would probably do him good. I don't think he gets out much, poor thing.)

So.

After Charlie did the snorting noise I decided to try a different approach. I put on my best quivery voice and said that he didn't know what it was like, having your mum and dad live apart and hardly ever seeing your dad because your mum's still angry about the time he invited nine of his mates round for a drink after a gig when she'd organised this posh dinner party and how I really missed him since he'd moved out and it was quite possible that I'd grow up Socially Disadvantaged as a result (I think that means you don't get invited on as many dates as people whose parents live together).

I even sniffed a bit (I can actually make myself cry real tears if I want, like a proper actress, but I have to go to the bathroom and poke myself quite hard in the eyes first).

Well.

At first I thought the quivery voice thing had done the trick (it ALWAYS works with Mum) because for a minute Charlie didn't say anything. He was sitting at the table by this time and he just stared down and picked at a bit of dried-on food with his fingernail. I thought he was probably really really moved by my story and was just about to agree to come with me after all, but he didn't say anything for so long that I started wondering if he'd heard. So I gave another big sniff and started saying 'you just don't know what it's - '

Well that did it, didn't it?

Charlie stopped staring at the bit of food and fixed me with this look. You've never seen anything like it. There were blue sparks of hate coming out of his eyes. And before I

knew what was happen-ing he started saying that it was ME who didn't know what it was like actually because he didn't have a dad AT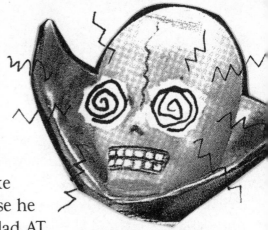
ALL and listening to me blethering on and on and on about how tough it is not to see mine every minute of every day of every week of every year was beginning to SERIOUSLY get on his nerves, so if I knew what was good for me I'd shut my big fat gob and leave him alone.

Well.

What would you have done?

Yup. That's what I did too.

I shut my big fat gob and left him alone.

That'll teach him.

Aaaaaaaaaaaaaaaaaaargh!!!!

Sorry. Had to do that. Just remembering it I can't help grinding my teeth together and making my jaw ache again.

Where does she get off? She has it so easy. I don't even know who my dad is. And there's her being all sniffy and pathetic. It just made me want to spit.

Aaaaaaaaaaaaaaaaaaargh!!!!

Sorry, just had to do it again.

My mate Johnny Ho's a Buddhist. His dad is, anyway. Johnny's more of a florist, cos his mum makes him work Saturdays in her flower shop. I asked him once what being a Buddhist was all about. His face went all twisty and weird, and I could tell he didn't really know, but what he did say was interesting. Something about nothing being really REAL, so not to get too excited about any of it.

'All things will pass,' he said, and I always remembered that. It kind of means that if you're having a GOOD

73

time it's not going to go on forever, no matter how much you want it to.

Which is BAD.

However.

When you're having a BAD time, that's not going to go on forever either.

Which is GOOD.

So, if you're going through a nightmare with an irritating, noisy, selfish girl who has the sensivity of an avalanche with an attitude problem, you shouldn't let it get you down too much because she'll eventually GO AWAY too.

And do you know what? They've got something, these Buddhists. Because she did. Go away, that is. And at long last the place was quiet.

I was glad she'd gone, but I was still absolutely steaming. I can't tell you how mad I was. There's no way I can write it down. I'd have to show you, and that wouldn't be very nice. I spent the next half-hour stamping up and down the kitchen, kicking things and growling. Then, when that was getting boring, I realised that there was nothing to stop me going to the match. Only I'd just spent half an hour stamping up and down the kitchen and it was too late. That made me even more furious, and I started kicking things again. But I stopped quicker this time. I didn't want to waste another half hour and miss the rugby.

That Janet ruins everything. Now I just wasn't in the mood. I was too twitchy to sit and watch TV. I needed to move around. I decided to go round to Johnny Ho's to see what he was up to.

I knew the way to the station all right so that was no problem. And I'd remembered to copy down the address of the place my dad was playing so I knew WHERE I was going. I just wasn't quite sure HOW I was going to get there.

The Crypt, Church St.

I was sure I could work it out though. I mean, how difficult could it be? People get to places they've never been before all the time.

Don't they?

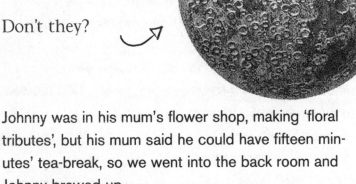

Johnny was in his mum's flower shop, making 'floral tributes', but his mum said he could have fifteen minutes' tea-break, so we went into the back room and Johnny brewed up.

Now, Johnny may be good with flowers, but what he wants to be when he grows up is a star of kung-fu movies. Not that he's any good at it. He's built less like a Chinese kung-fu expert than a Japanese sumo wrestler. That is, he's a bit on the plump side. Still, you've got to respect a guy who once tried to break a pile of bricks with his head, and now can't tell red from green. So I always listen to what he's got to say.

Except at traffic lights.

Johnny told me I mustn't turn my anger inwardly. I should give it free expression. He demonstrated by doing a kung-fu high kick.

Only it wasn't very high, and he kicked over a whole row of vases standing on the floor, breaking two of them.

Mrs Ho wasn't pleased. I tried to explain that Johnny was showing me how to give free expression to my anger, and she demonstrated how she gave free expression to hers by giving him a clip round the ear and sending him back to his flowers.

So I pushed off sharpish.

Anyway.

When I got to the station I bought a ticket from the machine (it's one of those titchy little stations that doesn't have a ticket office, so I just bought the cheapest one) and tried to decide which platform to wait on. There was no way of working it out, so in the end I decided I'd just go for the one with the most people on. That's usually quite a good sign.

Because if there's nobody going to a place then it's usually a pretty good indication that the place isn't worth going to.

And I knew that wherever my dad was playing was the kind of place that EVERYONE would want to go.

Once I got onto the platform I started to feel quite excited. There was this blind lady with a guide dog standing near me, so I started pulling faces at the dog. Dogs really like me. When I look at them they look right back into my eyes and I know that they're wishing they could come home with me and be MY dog instead of living with the person they do live with who probably keeps them in a shed and feeds them on nothing but sprouts and lumpy gravy.

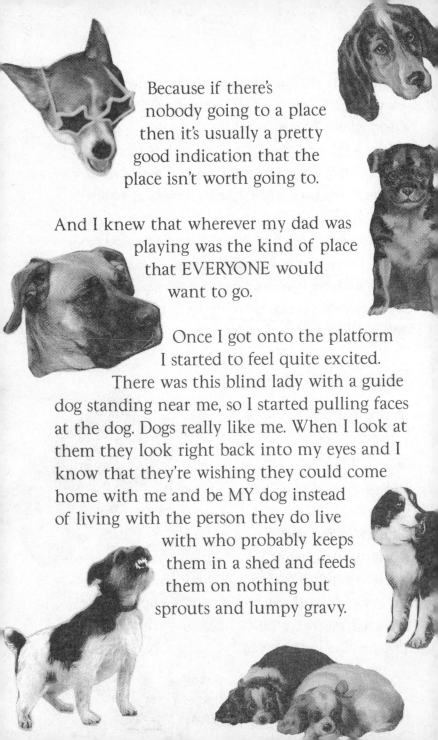

Well, it was the same with this dog.

He looked right at me and wagged his tail as if HE knew I was the kind of person who could find my way across town on my own, no trouble. All I had to do was get on the first train that came along and then ask some nice-looking person (the blind lady, for example) where I should get off. And once I'd done that all I had to do was get directions from a policeman or a traffic warden or someone and Bob's your uncle!

Easy peasy lemon squeezy.

And that got me thinking about how amazed Dad would be when I told him I'd come all this way on my own and how he'd give me one of his special hugs (the kind where he picks you up and whirls you round until you're sick) and then we'd sit down together and just talk and talk and talk.

And then of course he'd give me the

surprise.

I was getting so happy and excited just thinking about it that I completely forgot about having to get there first.

And then the train came.

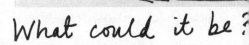

What could it be?

I just ended up wandering around. I thought about going to the cinema, but I didn't want to be out too late in case Deirdre and Geri got back. Anyway, it was too nice a day to sit indoors. Nice weather, anyway. I found an old can and kicked it down the road, imagining it was Janet, jumping and shouting 'Ow!' every time I did it. For some reason it cheered me up, and I started laughing. Kick. Ow! Ha ha. Kick. Ow! Ha ha. It even made me stop being mad at her. She didn't mean to be so annoying. She just couldn't help herself. And it was rough, not having a dad around. I knew.

I didn't think there was a chance she'd find him. She was probably standing at the wrong bus stop at that very moment. The thought of what a complete dipstick she was made me laugh even more. I took a long run up and gave the tin an almighty wallop. It sailed high in the air and disappeared over the railings of the bridge I was crossing. I peered over the edge, and there it was sitting right in the middle of the railway lines alongside platform two of the local railway station.

Well.

The blind lady and her dog and all the other people got on and I was just about to follow when it happened.

Somebody grabbed me by the back of my jacket and pulled me away just as the train doors were starting to close. It was SO embarrassing – I nearly fell over backwards and landed on my bum – all the people on the train were staring at me, including the blind lady and her dog. Well, her dog was, anyway.

Anyway, you can imagine how I felt.

I was furious. Whoever had done it had made me MISS MY TRAIN! I was just about to turn round and give them a big fat mouthful when I saw who it was.

Charlie.

That's right.

It was Charlie. . .

Chapter Six

You must sometimes wait for your heart's desire

Well, it was only the BRIGHTON train, wasn't it? If I'd have got on, I would have ended up miles away from home with no way of ever getting back and nothing to eat for the rest of my life but a very old cough drop that's been in my jacket pocket since prehistoric times.

So it was quite lucky that Charlie turned up when he did.

He SAID he'd only been passing by chance and just HAPPENED to spot me on the platform, but I could tell he was only saying that. I reckon he was really worried about me. Which made me feel. . .

Well, it got me thinking.

It got me thinking that maybe he'd been right when he told me to shut my big fat gob.

Maybe it had been a bit unfair to go on about my dad to somebody who didn't have a dad at all. Especially when I was only doing it to try and make that somebody come halfway across town with me to go and see my dad play at the wedding of some people he'd never met.

So do you know what I did?

I said. . .

Sorry

I just came straight out with it.

Because I was. Sorry, I mean.

And that's not all I did.

After I'd said sorry I told him that I only tried to persuade him to come with me because I was scared to go on my own!

I TOLD him!

How amazing is that?

I actually admitted I was scared!

And now I've admitted it again which makes it double amazing. In fact, now I come to think about it, I reckon that admitting you're scared is actually one of the BRAVEST things that anybody can do. It's far far braver than doing the sort of thing that seems brave to most people – like diving into a raging torrent full of flesh-eating piranhas to save a drowning baby or something. Because that actually isn't brave at all if you're a really good swimmer like me. It's just showing off.

But admitting to someone that you're scared. . .

That is TRULY brave.

Which must make me the bravest of the brave. Because I've done it TWICE.

I couldn't wait to tell Dad. (And Tiffani, of course. Because I tell her EVERYTHING).

I was totally gobsmacked! She said she was sorry! She actually apologised! I don't think anyone's ever done that to me before. Apart from that bloke who mugged Deirdre when we were Christmas shopping years ago. It must be hard NOT to say you're sorry when you've just nicked the train-set a little kid's been begging for all year. He might have been sorry, but he didn't give it back so I wasn't going to forgive HIM, ever.

But I forgave Janet. It had obviously been really difficult to say. In fact, her face twisted round into so many different shapes before she finally got it out, I very nearly burst out laughing. Which probably wouldn't have been the smartest thing to do. I think I handled the situation very well.

Somebody really has got to keep an eye on her, though. Sometimes she seems so massively USELESS. When I looked over the edge of the bridge, there she was happily standing with a crowd of holidaymakers just about to get on a train that would take her miles away. I must have broken several world records running across the bridge, and into the station in time to grab her.

At first it was like holding a cat over a bath, all teeth and claws. I was shouting at her that it was the wrong train, but she didn't take any notice. I thought she was going to take my arm off. When the train finally pulled out without her Janet swung round to hit me, but when she saw who it was she went all limp. And that's when she said it.

Anyway.

After we'd been through all that (I asked Charlie how he knew that train was going to Brighton and he said that all the families carrying beach balls and swimming things had been a bit of a giveaway. That and the fact it had BRIGHTON written on the front) we sort of relaxed. I asked him if he was going to come with me after all and he said he thought he better had, hadn't he, otherwise I'd end up in Merthyr Tydfil or somewhere else that was equally difficult to spell. And for some reason we both found this incredibly funny and just laughed and laughed and laughed until we realised that everyone on the platform was staring at us.

Everyone was staring at us.

So then we stopped and Charlie said that if we were going he'd better have a look at the directions, hadn't he, because I obviously didn't have a clue which way to go, so I dug them out of my pocket and showed him.

Well. That made him laugh even more, didn't it?

Because the place where my dad was playing was only ten minutes away!

AND

There was a train just pulling in to the opposite platform that would take us straight there! So what did we do?

89

We raced across to the other platform, scrambled onto the train seconds before it left, and collapsed in a big sweaty laughing heap on the seat, of course.

Mission accomplished.

Until we got to the other end. That was when things started to get SERIOUSLY difficult.

Well, it's not really surprising Janet almost caught the wrong train. What with her Dad's lousy directions, her terrible writing and all the finger prints, blobs of ink and the cough drop she'd managed to get on the little, grubby, crumpled bit of paper. All I could make out at first was 'Church Street'. Fat lot of use that was. There must be about a hundred Church Streets in every single town in the country.

I had to wet my thumb and rub hard before I could read where this wedding rave-up was supposed to be. Amazing! It was just two stops up the line. That kind of made my mind up. I was going too.

She can actually be quite a laugh when she wants to, Janet. When she's not being a complete pain, that is.

She had me howling on the train, telling me stories about Wizzo, her dad. Like the time he went to play a gig, walked on stage, opened his guitar case and a pile of knickers fell out. Apparently, Janet's mum had threatened to ground Dee if she didn't clean up her room, and she was too lazy to take her dirty clothes down to the wash-basket, so she'd just hidden them in the nearest receptacle. We had a real scream together on the journey, but it couldn't last. As soon as we rolled out of the station at the other end, Janet went back to her old self.

We had the address, you see, but we didn't have a map, so we just had to wander around hoping to spot the right street.

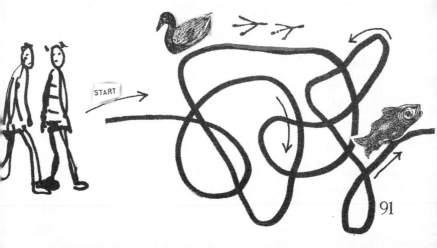

Well.

After we'd passed the same kebab shop for about the sixty-four million time I'd had enough. So I went and asked this policeman.

And guess what?

We'd only passed the street sixty-four million times already, hadn't we?

It was dead opposite the kebab shop.

92

I thought it was probably the road opposite the kebab shop with a church in it. I never got close enough to Janet to point that out. Every time I opened my mouth, she shot off again looking down this street or that alley, asking questions out loud then answering them herself all the time, like some demented parrot.

Eventually, after we'd been going round in circles for yonks, she stopped to ask a traffic warden. Surprise, surprise, it was the road I'd thought it was all along.

Well.

Once we were in the right street (thanks to ME, of course) it wasn't difficult to spot the place. It was this big churchy type building in

Janet

the middle of an overgrown graveyard – the sort of place I would've loved to play in when I was little – full of woodlice and tombstones and little stone angels with sad faces and broken wings.

I could have spent hours in there, just reading the names on the graves and poking the woodlice (I love the way they roll up into little balls like teeny miniature hedgehogs. Only without the prickles.

That was when I was little, of course. I am so past that now.

And anyway I didn't have the time to waste on dead people and woodlice and stuff. I wanted to see my dad. So I marched straight up to the main door of the building and tried the handle.

It's OK
it's not a real one!

And do you know what?

It was locked.

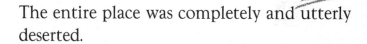

The entire place was completely and utterly deserted.

Once we got there, I was surprised to find I was looking forward to it. The gig, I mean. I didn't expect Janet's old man to be any GOOD, no matter what Janet said. He was probably just some old crusty who didn't know anything about proper music. But I'd never actually seen ANYBODY play live music before, and I've always quite fancied being a bit of an axe-hero myself. Once I've finished my international football career, of course.

Funnily enough, Janet didn't seem to be looking forward to it any more. In fact, as soon as she discovered the place was locked up, she started getting all twitchy and peculiar. She started rambling on about how I'd brought her to the wrong place, and how she knew it was really the other side of the kebab shop, and how it was going to rain and we were going to get soaked and we'd miss Wizzo and we'd never find our way home and all this stuff.

I told her to chill. Of course it was definitely the right place, cos there was a little piece of paper on the noticeboard by the gate saying 'Closed Saturday for Private Function', and this wedding bash was definitely a private function.

As for getting soaked, there were two small clouds in the sky. They couldn't have filled a kiddie's paddling pool between them. Janet wasn't having any, though, pacing up and down tugging at her hair so it was even more sticky-up than usual. At one point she even tried to drag me off towards the High Street to start searching again, but I put my foot down. I told her this was the place and I wasn't budging another inch. We were just a bit early, that's all. I don't think she really believed me, but then she got distracted making funny faces at this little old lady across the road who was cleaning her windows, and stopped driving me mad for a bit.

Charlie reckoned it wasn't such an incredibly big deal. Dad hadn't actually said what time the wedding started so we were probably just early and if we just sat down on the doorstep and waited, then someone would be sure to turn up.

I wasn't so sure. I kept worrying that maybe I'd got the wrong day or that Dad had given me the wrong address or that the people who were getting married had decided they didn't like each other after all and had cancelled the whole thing. And then it started to rain and this old woman in the house opposite kept looking at us from behind her curtains and then...

And then a van pulled up.

The door opened.

And my dad got out.

And everything was suddenly all right.

Chapter Seven

Someone you love will bring you joy

He looked just the same. Beat-up old leather jacket. Scruffy brown hair flopping over his face. And that special look that comes into his eyes when he looks at me and –

And –

AND –

HOORAY!!!!!!

He smelt the same too. A mixture of leather and soap and engine oil and something that doesn't smell like anything else in the world. And his chin was all spiky and the zip of his jacket dug into my chest and I couldn't breathe he was hugging me so tight and do you know what?

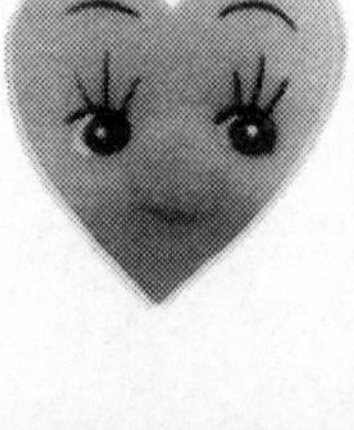

I didn't care.

Because I was in my dad's arms and he was spinning me round and for a second it was like the whole universe was holding its breath. . .

And then I remembered Charlie.

So this was Janet's dad. The one she'd been making so much fuss about. He didn't look like much to me.

OK. I'll admit it. I was a bit jealous. Janet was so happy, it reminded me of what I was missing. It was like she'd just met her absolutely best friend in the world, and that she loved him to death. Even if he was a bit stinky.

Well.

Charlie looked a bit weird and he kept on picking at this green stuff on one of the gravestones, but he shook hands and smiled politely when I introduced him to Dad.

I was just about to ask Dad about The Surprise when I noticed this other bloke hanging around. He had a ponytail and a stupid grin and when he saw me looking at him he said you don't remember me, do you, mush?

But I did.

It was only Mog, wasn't it?

Mog's the sound engineer. That means he has to drive the van, unload the gear and get the beers in at the end of the night before the pubs shut. Oh, and while Dad's on stage he messes about with some knobs and buttons and things at the back of the

room. That's to stop him getting bored, Dad says.

I used to really love Mog when I was little. I wasn't about to hug him though. He smells of compost.

Well.

After I'd finished telling Dad about how Charlie nearly got us lost and everything and we'd all stopped laughing, Mog looked at his watch and said we really ought to start on the get-in (that's a music business term that means unloading the van and GETTING all the gear IN to the church hall).

So while Mog was looking for the van keys, Charlie told Dad about the hall being locked up. Dad was just saying well, might as well go and wait down the pub then, when this grumpy looking man with a face like a smacked bum arrived jangling a big bunch of keys and let us into the hall.

We had arrived.

The next thing I know, the pair of them have pushed off, Janet in motormouth overdrive, leaving me with Mog, and I suddenly realise I'm expected to help him load all the stuff into the church hall. Great.

Actually, it didn't turn out so bad after all, cos there was all this interesting equipment like speakers and amps and pre-amps and mixing desks and stuff, and I learnt quite a lot about how it all goes together, and what it does.

Mog said he'd never really got on with Janet's mum. He reckoned Wizzo was better off without her. Maybe he was. But what about Janet? She certainly wasn't better off without her dad. Janet wasn't thinking about that right then, though. As we brought the last of the stuff in, she was still bending her dad's ear.

I can't tell you how great it was to see my dad again. It was like. . .

I know.

It was like when you've had a really horrible day at school when nothing's gone right and you feel like everyone hates you and you've tried to make friends but it's all come out wrong and your face is all stiff and aching from smiling too much and trying not to cry and then –

You go home.

You have your tea.

And you go to bed.

You snuggle down all lovely and warm under the duvet (maybe you've got a hot water bottle or a favourite teddy you've had since you were a baby or something) where no-one can get at you or tell you off or laugh at you behind your back and you just re-e-e-lax . . .

Big hug.

Of course, I'm way past that now, but it's what I feel like when I see my dad, you know?

Anyway. The first thing I did when we got in the hall was ask him about The Surprise. And do you know what he said?

He said. . .

WAIT AND SEE

Usually I hate it when grown-ups say that. But Dad explained how it would spoil the surprise if he told me now, so I tried my best to forget about it and got on with telling him all about my new school and Daisy Micklepage and how she didn't believe I had a dad who was a rock star and everything. I was JUST getting round to asking him about the Stars for a Night thing when this woman with mad hair arrived. She was in a total panic and started going on about the guests arriving any

minute and how she'd never get the
food out in time and she was buzzing
around the room so much I thought she
was going to explode. So when Dad said why
didn't me and Charlie give her a hand while
he went off to get ready, I felt so sorry for
her that I agreed.

Well.

It didn't seem much like party food to me –
loads of boring old salads and stuff – but
Charlie said that's what these kind
of grown-ups like. There was a
wedding cake though, a
really huge one, which
had Barbie and Ken on
the top instead of
the usual boring old
bride and groom. So that
was quite cool.

Anyway.

By the time we'd finished and I
was just getting round to having

another go at asking Dad about Stars for a Night, the wedding guests had started to arrive. They all seemed incredibly over-excited – like a bunch of five-year-olds at a birthday party – all shouting and laughing and kissing each other so I got a bit distracted and forgot all about it again.

Well.

I was just eating my third bit of cake and watching this bloke with dreadlocks trying to balance an empty champagne bottle on his nose when there was this big cheer and Dad walked on stage. I looked round to see what had happened to Charlie because I didn't want him to miss one second, but I couldn't see him in the crush of cheering bodies so –

And then Dad
started to play
and I didn't
think about
anything
any more.

Wow!

Everybody seemed to be having a great time, stuffing their faces and shouting, but I was getting really fed up. I'd only come along to keep an eye on Janet, and I'd been dragged into doing all the work, shifting stuff and laying tables. And I was beginning to feel a bit uncomfortable, because it was getting late. I was sure Deirdre would be home by now and wondering what had happened to us. I didn't want her thinking we'd been kidnapped or something.

So I phoned her, just so she wouldn't worry. Big mistake. She told me to stay right where I was, and she'd come out to get us immediately. I begged her not to. Told her we could get back on our own no problem, but she wasn't having any. At least I got her to promise not to tell Janet's mum. We didn't want a fight at the wedding.

The party was in full swing by now, with the bride leading the dancing. They were a really noisy bunch. But I couldn't stop watching the door. The trip should have taken Deirdre at least an hour, what with getting to the station and everything, but you can never tell with her.

So, I wasn't paying too much attention when the

record finished and Wizzo came on. I was still looking nervously at the door. Then there was this HUGE cheer, and he started, and do you know what? He was brilliant! And I don't mean just ordinary brilliant. He was a one-man party! In seconds the hall was heaving. Nobody was sitting except one bloke who had his leg in plaster, and even he was jigging up and down. I wouldn't have believed it if I hadn't see it with my own eyes. Janet was right. Her dad was a star. Mog gave me a little wink, and I couldn't help but smile back. The music just did that to you. I was having such a good time, I forgot all about the phone call. . .

The hall was so full of people drinking and dancing and shouting and I was so into watching my dad that I didn't notice her at first. And when I did I thought I must be mistaken. She was standing in the doorway peering into the crowd of gyrating bodies as if she was trying to find someone. And then I saw her heading over to Charlie and realised it was no mistake.

It was Charlie's mum.

I couldn't believe it. At first I thought it must

be some weird coincidence – maybe she'd been invited to the wedding as well, maybe –

And then I realised. It was no coincidence. Charlie had phoned her. He'd ASKED her to come.

Well, you can imagine how THAT made me feel. Just when I'd been thinking that MAYBE he wasn't as bad as all that and MAYBE we could ALMOST be friends, what does the ickle baby diddums do? He sneaks off and phones his mummy and tells her where we are so she can come and pick us up and take us home to beddy-byes before my dad's even finished playing!

I hated him. I really really hated him.

What's more, you can bet your bottom dollar that the first thing Weirdre Deirdre did when her little boy called was to go knocking on MY door and dob me in to MY mum. So when I got home

Charlie

she'd be waiting, ready to kill me or inflict
unimaginable punishments on me for the rest
of my life.

The crime scene

And probably
never ever let me go
and see my dad ever
again.

Well, I wasn't going to put up
with THAT, was I?

I thought Deirdre was going to give me hell at first,
but in fact, she was quite pleased. She was pleased
I'd been sensible enough to call her, and she was

pleased because this looked like a fun do. Apparently, Geri was fine, but they were keeping her in overnight just to make sure all the buttons had come out, so as far as Deirdre was concerned, she was free to party, and Deirdre is a PARTY ANIMAL. She'd even brought transport, so there was a lift home. Things weren't working out so badly after all.

And then I realised.

I didn't have to put up with it. I didn't have to go home. Because unlike some people I could mention I've actually got more than one parent. I've got a DAD.

Big Idea

And I could stay with him.

Perfect.

So as soon as Dad had finished playing his first set (to huge rounds of applause and screams for more, naturally) I rushed backstage to ask him.

And do you know what he said?

He said. . .

no.

Chapter Eight

Someone you love will cause you pain

I kept wanting to dance, and that is just so not cool. Dancing's for girls and old people. I had to hang onto the side of the sound desk, watching what Mog was up to and trying to stop my feet doing their own thing. Nothing was going to stop Deirdre, though. She was dancing like a lunatic with everyone else in the room, especially the bride. None of them seemed bothered that they didn't know her. Adults are weird.

No.

He said no.

NO!

I couldn't believe it.

My own father wouldn't let me stay with him. Not even for one stupid little night. Oh, he made some useless excuse about having to go off on tour first thing tomorrow morning and not being there to make sure I got home all right and how Mum wouldn't like it at this short notice anyway, but that he'd talk to her when he got back and THEN we'd spend some proper time together. . .

But he couldn't fool me. Not any more. I knew it was all complete and utter rubbish.

The truth was he didn't want me.

My own father didn't want me.

Well, I suppose I shouldn't have been surprised. It was nothing new. I mean if Dad had REALLY wanted me then he and Mum would never have split up, would they? He would've made more of an effort to patch things up so he could stay living with me. But he didn't want to. Just like everybody else. Mum's always been too busy or tired to talk or do anything with me and Dee can't tell me often enough how much she hates my guts. And no-one at school has EVER wanted to be friends with me, not really. Even Tiffani (remember her? The one with the big house and the brother who fancies me?) isn't a real friend. Because she's not a real person. I made her up.

There. I said it.

I MADE TIFFANI UP.

Which meant that the only friend I had in the world was an imaginary one. How sad is that?

Apart from Charlie, of course, but he didn't count. Not now he'd sneaked on me behind my back. A TRUE friend wouldn't do that. I was just kidding myself when I thought he wanted to be my friend. He never really wanted to have anything to do with me. Just like all the others.

Just like Dad. . .

In fact, now I came to think of it, that was

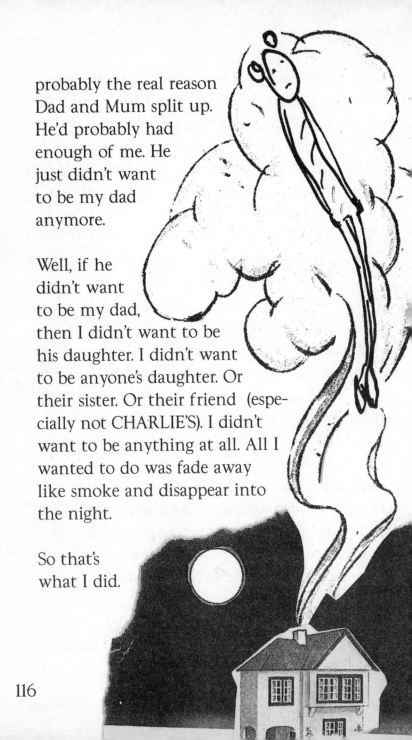

probably the real reason
Dad and Mum split up.
He'd probably had
enough of me. He
just didn't want
to be my dad
anymore.

Well, if he
didn't want
to be my dad,
then I didn't want to be
his daughter. I didn't want
to be anyone's daughter. Or
their sister. Or their friend (especially not CHARLIE'S). I didn't
want to be anything at all. All I
wanted to do was fade away
like smoke and disappear into
the night.

So that's
what I did.

116

While everybody was dancing and singing and having an utterly fantastic time I just slipped out the door of the hall into the darkness.

And do you know what?

Nobody noticed I'd gone.

They were all having too much fun.

One song after another, Wizzo just belted them out, and everybody cheered, like they knew them all. The crowd was dancing so hard, you could actually feel the wooden floor of the hall bouncing up and down.

A good job he wrapped it up when he did, though, cos some of the really old ones looked like they might have to be carried out if he'd gone on much longer. Even so, everyone screamed 'More! More! More!', and they only calmed down when he said he'd do just one more song. A special song. Something he'd been saving as a surprise. This one, he said, is for the most important person in my life. And guess who that was? Here's a clue. It was called 'Janet's song'.

Aha! That was THE SURPRISE! I looked around for

her everywhere. I bet she was as pink as a poodle's ribbon, but I couldn't spot her. Probably hiding from embarrassment because the song was really slow and gooey. It started:

> *I guess I've not been much of a dad to you*
> *I've been on the road for too long*
> *You must miss me, and I miss you too*
> *So I wrote about you in a song*

See what I mean? Mog leaned over and whispered to me that he was recording a tape of it, specially for Janet, and could I give it to her after? As I nodded, Wizzo suddenly stamped the floor four times and the song speeded right up. This was more like it! In no time at all, everyone was dancing again, and singing along with the chorus:

> *There will never be another Janet*
> *More than diamonds she's worth*
> *You may think she's from another planet*
> *But she's the best girl here on Earth.*

It turned out to be the best song of the night. In fact, the dancing wrinklies liked it so much, they made him play it again.

When he'd finally finished, to a huge great cheer, Deirdre came over, all hot and sweaty and said it really was time we were off, otherwise Kate might start worrying. I got the tape from Mog, and went off to find Janet to tell her we had a lift. I thought she was probably behind the stage with Wizzo, but she wasn't. He hadn't seen her. And neither had anyone else.

I didn't know where I was going and I didn't care either. So I just walked. First, I headed back to the main street and found myself outside the kebab shop. The street was quite busy with cars and taxis and loads of people eating stuff and laughing and waiting at bus stops. But I didn't feel like hanging around. I just wanted to keep moving. So I put my head down and set off, away from all the shops and all the people. It was starting to rain a bit, but I didn't care.

And you know, there was something comforting about it in a way. Being out alone in the city at night I mean. With the night buses rumbling past and the police sirens going in the distance and the car headlights reflecting on the wet tarmac and the glow in the sky

119

from all the street lamps, looking like a huge orange dome completely covering the entire city and keeping it all safe and cosy and warm. . .

It was all so big and I was so small and at first I really liked that. It made me feel like my problems didn't matter. It made me feel like nothing mattered actually. I just walked along watching my feet on the wet pavement – left right, left right, don't stand on the cracks or you'll get a fright. . .

And then I did.

Get a fright, I mean. A big one.

ARGHHHH!

It's surprising how many different little rooms and cupboards there are in those old halls. We looked everywhere, Deirdre and me, shouting for Janet, but no reply. It took ages. There was a cupboard full of different types of balls, and one full of baby's toys. But no Janet.

There was a kitchen with the biggest collection of unmatching cups and saucers you could imagine, and a huge tea-urn that looked like an unexploded bomb. No Janet there, either.

There was an old wooden ladder that led to an upstairs room as big as the main hall which was completely full of dusty clothes. Janet could have hidden in hundreds of places. But she hadn't. She wasn't there.

There was a creaky old staircase diving down into a black, smelly cellar where the light didn't work. I don't think she was down there. I called, but I wasn't going to go down to find out. Deirdre wasn't keen either.

That left just one place. She had to be in the hall. We must have missed her in the crowd of dancers.

I'd got quite a distance from the kebab shop by this time and there were less people about. But it was still quite bright from the street lights and there was loads of traffic around so I wasn't worried. I wasn't even worried when I saw this big lumpy thing in the doorway of a boarded up shop. I thought it was a heap of old rags and was just about to prod it with my foot when it moved. It shifted on the ground as if it was alive and then, without warning, it reared up at me like a dragon in a fairy-tale and ROARED.

Well.

For a split second I couldn't move. My stomach did this horrible lurchy thing and the street seemed to wriggle like a worm. And then I started to run. I know now that I'd just woken up some poor old bloke who was sleeping rough in the shop doorway, but I didn't then. I was terrified.

So I ran. I didn't know where I was going. I just ran.

I ran and I ran and I ran. . .

It was like trying to find one particular kid in a big toy shop on Christmas Eve. The place was really heaving. I was sure there were even more of them than before. I tried to ask this one woman if she'd seen Janet, and she just wrapped her arms around me and started dancing, pressing me hard into her chest, so I could hardly breathe. It was well gross. I'd just managed to pull myself away when Deirdre grabbed me. A recent arrival had seen Janet heading off down the street. She was somewhere out there in the city. Deirdre was very worried. She had friends in this area. It wasn't a good part of town to be alone in at night.

When I finally stopped running I found myself in a completely different sort of area. It was probably quite nice in daytime, in a boring sort of way, the sort of place where Mum would love us to live, full of proper houses with little front gardens and hedges and stuff, but at night it was a different matter. It wasn't all busy and bright like the other streets, with buses trundling past and people eating kebabs and old blokes sleeping in shop doorways. There were no buses, no cars and no people. Just rows and rows of houses all with their lights off or their curtains closed tight against the night.

And I knew.

I knew that ANYTHING could happen to me in this street. I could yell, or shout for help, or scream my head off, or even go and hammer on one of the neat front doors and beg them to let me in because something was after me – I don't know what it is but I know it's horrible and I know it's out to get me and it's coming closer and closer and closer – I can see its long black shadow stretching out towards me along the pavement and hear its footsteps getting nearer – thump, thump, thump, thump – and now I can hear its breathing – wheezing and puffing

THUMP!

GRUNT

PUFF

WHEEZE

like an old man climbing the stairs – coming closer, closer, closer – so close now that I can smell it and it stinks of filth and death and rotting corpses and I can feel its breath on the back of my neck and –

PUFF

And nobody would take a blind bit of notice. They'd all just sit there on their big fat bottoms in front of their stupid TV's and pretend they couldn't hear anything at all because whatever was going on outside in the street was NOTHING TO DO WITH THEM.

And all of a sudden I felt horribly alone. The city didn't feel like a big warm friendly animal any more and I didn't feel like I was part of it. It felt like a cold dead soulless place where I could die of misery right there on the pavement and nobody would even notice let alone care. And I didn't know what to do. So I sat down on the pavement and started to cry. I was lost. I was cold. I was frightened.

And I realised that I didn't really care about Daisy or the Stars for a Night thing or any of that stuff. There was only one thing I cared about and that was the one thing I couldn't have right now.

My mum.

mum

I wanted my mum.

Janet could have been anywhere. When me and Deirdre left the church hall we weren't feeling very hopeful at all. We didn't have a clue where to start looking. We just had to start. Only, there was one other not-so-small complication, as I realised when we got outside the churchyard.

When Deirdre'd said she had transport, I should have been suspicious then. She had only one friend who was likely to trust her with his wheels, and he wasn't exactly your average family saloon driver.

I stared up at the monster with my mouth open, before Deirdre yelled at me to get a move on, and I climbed on board.

Across the dashboard in big sparkly letters was the name – 'PEGASUS'. Gandolfo called it his trusty steed. Now I'm no expert, but even I know that Pegasus was supposed to be some big white horse with wings. This thing was no flying horse. It was thirty feet of stinking old diesel bus. With no seats. But full of carpets and cushions and curtains and… well, just STUFF. Loads of stuff. It even had a cooker. And a stereo with a set of speakers about five times the size of Mog's. And five times as loud, as I soon found out when Deirdre started the engine. A noise came blasting out that sounded like somebody having their teeth drilled under water.

'It's well, music!' Deirdre shouted over the racket. It didn't sound like any kind of music to me, well or not, but she repeated it and I realised she'd said 'Whale music'. Which is whales talking really, but old hippies like Gandolfo think any squeaky noise that really means 'Those pilchards were past their sell-by date' is music. 'Can't work out how to turn it off,' she yelled, and floored the accelerator, leaving the church hall behind in a cloud of filthy black smoke as I desperately looked for a button or switch or ANYTHING to turn off that horrible noise. No luck. We were stuck with it.

You wouldn't have thought things could get any worse, would you?

But they did.

There I was sitting on the pavement crying my eyes out when I heard this noise. It was a roaring, blaring, rumbling noise like nothing I'd ever heard. And I looked up and saw these incredibly bright white lights heading towards me. The noise was getting louder and the lights were getting closer and –

129

Chapter Nine

You will discover that things are not always what they seem

Now there are various different ways to find somebody who's lost. The best is to get a dog to sniff that person's old socks or something, then follow their scent. The second best is probably to get loads of people with maps to walk down every street until they've covered the whole area. The worst is to look for them in a bus driven by someone with no sense of direction, and which is so noisy you can't hear yourself think. You'd have to be really lucky for that to work.

Guess what. We were lucky.

Guess what. It wasn't a monster or a space ship or a Ghost Truck from Hell. It was Charlie and his weirdo mother in some stupid hippy bus she'd borrowed off a friend.

I was glad they'd found me, of course.

Glad I wasn't going to have to spend the night in that horrible scary street. Glad I was going home to Mum.

STUPID But I was also feeling really really stupid.

Think about it. I'd run away like some silly little kid. I'd made Charlie and his mum go driving round the streets looking for me. I'd mistaken a sad old bloke for a dragon and a stupid hippy bus for a space ship. And my dad wasn't going to play at the school on Monday so I was going to be totally humiliated by Daisy Micklepage in front of everybody.

That's enough to make ANYONE feel stupid.

Even me.

She was sitting on the pavement under a lamppost in this really bozo road. It was the kind of street where nobody ever goes out. They just sit indoors and com-plain about other people. Ha, ha! We certainly gave

131

them something to complain about. You could see all the curtains moving a little bit as we came roaring along blasting out whale music and lighting up the whole road. Did I mention the lights? Gandolfo was obviously mad keen on them, so the bus was covered. About twenty headlights. Spots on the roof. Strips of little red and green bulbs that lit one after the other along the sides. Flickery electric candles in the windows. A little luminous Buddha figure hanging in the doorway. There were even purple fluorescents underneath to light up the road! This was one bus nobody could miss!

Janet looked like a rabbit caught in a . . . well, in a headlight. She peered up at the bus, rain all over her face, eyes and mouth wide open. She looked scared, but once she realised who it was I reckoned she'd be really pleased to see us. I stuck my head out of the door as Deirdre pulled to a stop and I yelled, 'Taxi, madam?'

She didn't laugh.

I got in.

Well, I had no choice, did I? I could hardly pretend I was waiting at a bus stop or going to see a friend or collecting money for Homeless Dolphins or something. It was the middle of the night, it was pouring with rain and I was sitting on the pavement crying my eyes out. So I got in. Deirdre made some joke about the weird people you come across on the streets these days and we were off.

Charlie kept blethering about the gig, but I didn't say anything. Partly because I was listening to these amazing sounds coming out of the speakers but mostly because I just wanted to get home. Even though I knew that the moment I walked in the door I'd have to face something that was much scarier than anything I'd been up against so far.

I'd have to face my mum.

Janet didn't say a word for the entire journey, and when we got back, she ran straight to her own flat and that was the last I saw of her until Monday morning.

I was right, of course. Mum was waiting up for me when I got back. The moment I got to the front door it flew open and there she was, looking – not mad as I expected – but all sort of blotchy and weird. And then, instead of shouting at me like I thought she would, she just went, 'Oh Janet. I was so – ' and then gulped and gave me a hug. So that was all right.

Me and my mum

It got better too.

Because then we went indoors, and she made hot chocolate and we had a Talk. Usually having a Talk is a real pain because it means HER talking about something I'VE done wrong and ME not being allowed to say anything because that's Answering Back. But this time was different.

Mum still did most of the talking but it wasn't all about me. It was about her. It turned out that Deirdre hadn't told her everything about me and Charlie sneaking off on our own, but

(as she said) it didn't
take a genius to work out where we'd gone.
And that had got her thinking and she'd
decided it wasn't really fair to stop me
seeing Dad. Just because she and him had
their problems it didn't mean I should
suffer. Then she said she was going to
ring him up first thing and get him
to make some regular arrangement
to take me out. Like every
Saturday or something. How cool
was that?

Well, it WAS pretty cool and it DID make me
feel quite a bit better. But not as much as
you'd think. Partly because there was no
guarantee that Dad would go along with it
(he's not really the most reliable of people.
Mum's right about that) but mostly because I'd
just looked at the time and realised it was
gone midnight. Which meant –

I couldn't bear to think about what it meant
actually, so I decided to e-mail Tiffani instead.
That's usually what I do to cheer myself up.

To: Tiffani
From: Janet
Subject: Weekend Fun

How was your weekend? Mine was incredible! I
went to see my dad playing at this really amazing –

Except it didn't work this time. I couldn't kid
myself any longer. My weekend had been
horrible, my life was the pits and my best
friend didn't exist.

And it was Sunday morning. Which meant
that it was Monday tomorrow.

And on Monday it was the show.

While we were walking into school together I tried to tell her how much I'd enjoyed our adventure and how brill I thought Wizzo had been but she just muttered 'yeah' without being very enthusiastic. I thought maybe she was annoyed about having to come home in Pegasus and said I was sorry about that but how it was Deirdre's idea, not mine, and anyway, it was probably better than having to walk miles home in the rain. She just said 'yeah' again, and carried on staring at the pavement and kicking at invisible stones. I didn't get anything out of her all the way to school, and when we got there, she just sat at her desk in class, staring out the window.

Still, I had other things to think about. It was the day of the Stars for a Night gig, and I was stage manager. That means being in charge. I had to do all the stuff like opening and closing the tabs (that's curtains to you non-stage-managers), telling people when it's their turn to go on, turning the lights on and off and getting all the props ready – props are anything they carry – swords, magic wands, banjos – we even had a live kitten when I did the Christmas show.

There wasn't much of this for the Stars for a Night show, obviously. Mainly the tabs and the lights and seeing what order everybody had to go on, but I needed to check everything was working all right, especially the sound system. It was enough to think about, so I forgot all about Janet. For the time being.

I thought about it all day. During assembly, during lessons, while I was eating my dinner. I have packed lunch, but I was sitting with some of the people who have school dinners. There's Rosie, who was one of the few people who was nice to me on my first day, and Yemi and Sean, and they were all being really friendly. But I didn't feel like talking. All I could think about was the show. I knew I was never going to be able to prove my Dad WAS a rock star so the only way to avoid total humiliation was to stop Daisy getting there in the first place.

But how?

I was just working on a plan to tie her up with her hair bands and lock her in the girls' toilets when it happened:

'Ooh look! It's Daddy's Girl!'

She had her two cronies with her, one either side, and was looking well pleased with herself.

'Is your famous daddy coming along to play tonight, then?'

I opened my mouth to reply, but before I could get a word out, she'd picked up one of my sandwiches and looked inside.

'So what've we got here, Daddy's Girl? Peanut butter? How sad! I would've thought your mummy could afford something better than that. What with your dad being a ROCK STAR and everything.'

I didn't say anything. I couldn't. I was too furious.

She dropped my sandwich, then looked across at the other people on the table and raised her voice so they could all hear:

'Never mind! You can always get your mum to apply for free school dinners next term. I'm sure you'd be eligible. What with your mum being a SINGLE PARENT and everything. Then you'll fit right in with all the other sad-dos!'

I couldn't believe she said that. I could not believe it. I mean I knew she was a pig, but...

P-G
D---Y

Rosie looked like she was going to cry. I put my hand on her arm and turned to tell Daisy what I thought of her but she'd already gone, shaking her hair and laughing with her horrible friends.

I looked down at my peanut butter sandwich. And I felt like I was going to throw up.

I knew there had to be something really wrong with Janet when I saw how she reacted to Daisy. I'd have expected her to give as good as she got, as usual, but she just sat there and took it, and Daisy flounced off with her nose in the air, looking well pleased with herself in that way that makes you long for a bucketful of dog-puke and rat-snot to come magically tumbling out of nowhere and land right on her head.

I was steaming. I don't like to get mixed up in other people's fights, but me and Janet were almost, well, a little bit, friends, and I DO get mixed up in friends' fights. You ask Johnny Ho. When he got set on by those two oiks from the next year, didn't I get stuck in? We did pretty well too. Johnny got a cracking kung-fu kick in on Len Wallace's metal toe-cap, and I totally crushed Spiz Cudley's pasty. That was before they flattened us of course.

141

Trouble is, you can't go round picking fights with girls. They just scream and get you in real trouble. I needed to think of something else. I didn't have time, though. I had to get the stage ready for the show.

Then it all just fell into my lap. Guess who turned up demanding special attention while I was testing the tabs?

Yes? You guessed. Miss 'I'm the most wonderful girl in the world' Daisy Micklepage. Apparently the video of the song she was doing showed her favourite pop star flying through the air in a superhero costume. I'd seen it. It was rubbish. Her mother had bought her a copy of the costume specially, and now Daisy was after a favour from me.

You see, there'd been a fairy in the Christmas show. A flying fairy. It had really just been a bit of rope hanging over a bar with the fairy on it and four kids holding the other end out of sight of the audience, but it hadn't looked bad. Daisy wanted to do it again, and she wanted me to sort it out for her. Me!

I was just about to tell her to take her superhero costume and stuff it... when I had a thought. And then another. And another. And I had a really hard job stopping myself from smirking.

'Of course I'll sort it out for you, Daisy,' I said. 'It'll be my pleasure.'

Well, that was it, really. The End of the Story. I decided it was about time I faced up to reality. There was no way I could stop Daisy from going to the show and there was no way I could avoid total humiliation. And it was all my fault for boasting about Dad. So I made a resolution. I was going to change. From now on I was going to stop making things up and exaggerating and trying to make my life more exciting than it really was. I was going to be like everyone else. I was going to be ORDINARY.

the end
the end
the end the end
the end
the end
the end
the end.

And I wasn't going to go to the show tonight. I was going to stay at home and mail Tiffani one last time.

To: Tiffani
From: Janet
Subject: You

I know it's silly writing to someone who doesn't
exist but I've been doing it for so long that I
almost believe you do. I can picture your lovely big
house with its lawns and flower beds and tennis
courts as clear as anything and if I try really hard
I can see you standing there on the grass by the
front door. You're wearing a white dress and
you've got dark wavy hair and dear old Bob, your
faithful golden retriever, is lying at your feet. I
can't see your face though, no matter how hard I
concentrate. But you're waving and waving and
waving and I'm about to wave back and go running
towards you when suddenly I realise. You're not
waving hello like you usually do. You're waving
goodbye.

Goodbye Tiffani. You've been a good best friend.
One day I might even get a real one.

Love
Your friend

Carmen Amaretto del Fuego Delafonte Passionflower
Poisson.
(AKA JANET).

Chapter Ten

You will find true happiness through a good friend

Guess what?

I ended up going after all. To the Stars for a Night thing, I mean. I'd just finished my last e-mail to Tiffani and was turning off the computer when there was a knock at the kitchen door. I quickly stuffed the print-out of my note in my knicker drawer along with all the others. I didn't want to see anyone, I just wanted to hide.

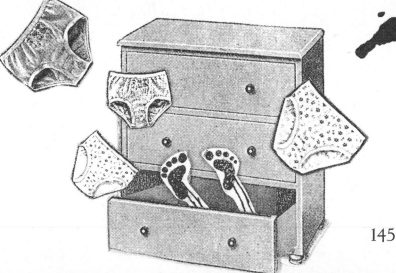

But whoever it was, wasn't about to give up.

Go Away .

Knock knock.

Go Away

Knock knock.

Go

Then a wonderful thought popped into my head. A thought that made all the horrible-ness of the last couple of days disappear like smoke. . .

What if Dad had felt really really guilty when he heard about me running away during the show?

What if he'd managed to cancel his tour?

146

And what if he'd decided to come and play at the school after all and had made up with Mum and was standing there outside my bedroom door just waiting to give me the good news and sweep me up into his arms?

Well, you can imagine. With that lovely thought in my head I just flew across the room and threw open the door and. . .

It wasn't him.

You didn't really think it would be, did you?
Things like that never actually happen, not
when you've imagined them anyway.

So who was it then?

I'll give you three guesses.

Charlie. Charlie. Charlie.

That's right. It was Charlie.

CHarlie

I knew I'd never get her to go on her own. I needed to
bring in the big guns. I needed her mum to MAKE her
go. For that, I had to get Deirdre's help. And the only
way to do that was to tell her my plan.

I knew it was a winner as soon as I saw the big smile
on her face.

The best thing about my mum is that once she's on
your side she'll move heaven and earth for you. That's
exactly what she did.

She marched straight down to Janet's flat and started telling her mum how I'd never had any friends (ha ha!) and how it would be so NICE if Janet would go along to keep me company, because I'd be so LONELY otherwise.

I stood behind her looking very, very sad, which was very, very difficult cos I really wanted to laugh my head off, but Janet's mum lapped it all up. She said she understood entirely, and it would do Janet good to go out and have fun with the rest of the kids from school.

When I banged on J's door to tell her to get her coat she gave me a look that would have knocked over a charging rhino, but it was too late. The battle was already won. She'd thank me later.

I refused, of course. Why would I want to go and be humiliated in front of the whole school? (And why would Charlie want me to? The whole thing was getting way too weird for my liking.) So I said no. I said I wasn't going and nobody could make me and that was that.

Then Mum dropped her bombshell.

She said that if I didn't go she wasn't going to phone Dad in the morning like she promised.

Well.

I had no choice then, did I? Not when she said that. I had to go.

So there I was. Standing there at the back of the school hall along with a hundred or so other kids and a few of the teachers. There'd already been a couple of acts – mostly wannabes singing along to tapes of their favourite pop songs and now some saddo from Year Nine was playing 'When the Saints Go Marching In' on his clarinet.

It was so terrible that the whole audience had given up pretending to listen and were starting to chat amongst themselves. I could see Rosie and Yemi trying not to laugh and Mr Walker looked like he was trying to sneak out the door without anyone noticing. I could tell I wasn't the only one who was beginning to wonder why I'd bothered to come.
And I couldn't see Charlie anywhere. He'd disappeared off as soon as we'd arrived, to do

whatever it is stage managers do, I supposed. Or to get away from Clarinet Boy. I couldn't see Daisy either, which was one tiny ray of sunshine. Though I was sure it was only a matter of time before she'd arrive with her cronies and start making sneery comments about my dad and get me all upset and then I'd lose my temper and start shouting and everybody would stare and –

That was when I decided to go home.

And then it happened.

Oh when the saints (OH WHEN THE SAINTS!)
Go marching in (Go MARCHING IN!)
Oh when the saints go marching in.
Da da da da, da da da da.

Was I looking forward to this, or what? Specky Dave had finally strangled the last note out of his clarinet and the big moment was coming fast. I closed the tabs and my four 'fairy-fliers' sprang into action, tying Miss Wannabe Micklepage onto the end of her rope. She was dressed head to foot in silver satin, with a cape and boots just like the singer in the video. She looked a right pillock. At least the mask covered her

151

stuck-up nose. She was so busy giving her helpers a hard time about keeping their grubby little hands off her cape, she didn't see Johnny Ho come sneaking onto the stage behind me. I looked a question at him, and with the biggest smirk you've ever seen he lifted up the can I'd asked him to bring. Great!

First though, a little surprise for someone out there in the audience. I threw Daisy's tape in the bin and slipped the tape I had in my pocket into the machine instead. Then I pressed the start button and turned it up nice and loud.

I was halfway out the door when a voice came over the speakers. It was really loud but not the kind of loud that hurts your ears. This was a soft, warm sort of loud that filled the room like honey and vibrated inside me.

It seemed to have a similar effect on everybody else in the room as well. I could see Rosie and Yemi and Sean with their mouths hanging open and Mr Walker staring as if he'd seen a ghost. And it was the same all round the hall. Everybody had stopped whatever they were doing and was listening to that voice.

Guess who it was?

That's right.

It was my dad.

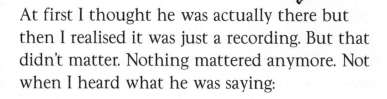

At first I thought he was actually there but then I realised it was just a recording. But that didn't matter. Nothing mattered anymore. Not when I heard what he was saying:

OK everyone, I want you all to listen up because the next song is a particularly special one for me. That's because I wrote it for a particularly special person who just so happens to be in the room with us tonight. She might not know who she is right now but she will in a minute because the song's called Janet's Song and it's for my lovely daughter. I love you, Janet. This is for you.

I looked around to see if Daisy Micklepage was there. She had to hear this, she had –
And then Dad started to sing and I stopped caring about Daisy Micklepage. I stopped caring about everything.

Because I had a song. A song that my Dad had written for me. A song that was MINE.

It was Janet's Song.

And I loved it.

The whole audience were singing along before Daisy realised what was going on. It was too late by then. She was tied in tight, and at my signal, the lads, who were cheerfully warbling along as well, hoisted her off the ground and she was totally stuck. She screamed and swore and threatened all kinds of horrible things if we didn't let her down, but nobody in the audience could hear a thing with all the singing.

Daisy screamed even louder when Johnny showed her what was in the can. Blue paint. Not pale blue like babies' cardigans, or navy blue like school uniform, but ROYAL blue. The colour of the sky in the evening after a really sunny day, when the sun's gone down but it's not completely dark yet. You know?

A good slosh of blue on the bum and a firm shove on the rope and dear Daisy was bouncing from wall to wall, leaving lovely blue butterflies wherever she hit.

Whenever she slowed down the lads gave the rope a tug to get her going again, or Johnny prodded her with a stick. I'm not one to boast, but it was a very, very proud moment. I can also honestly say that when I opened the tabs so that the whole school could gaze with wonder at the screaming, blue-in-the-face and blue-on-the-bum WonderWally, it was the happiest moment of my life.

In fact, just thinking about it now makes me want to laugh so much I might wet myself. I'd better go.

To: Tiffani
From: Janet
Subject: You #2

Forget that last letter. It was rubbish. You do exist, this isn't goodbye and we're still gonna be best friends forever. (Even though I have got another friend now. His name's Charlie and I THINK you're going to like him).

Oh, and by the way, my name's not Janet.

It's Carmen Amaretto del Fuego Delafonte Passionflower Poisson.

And I'm EXTRAORDINARY.

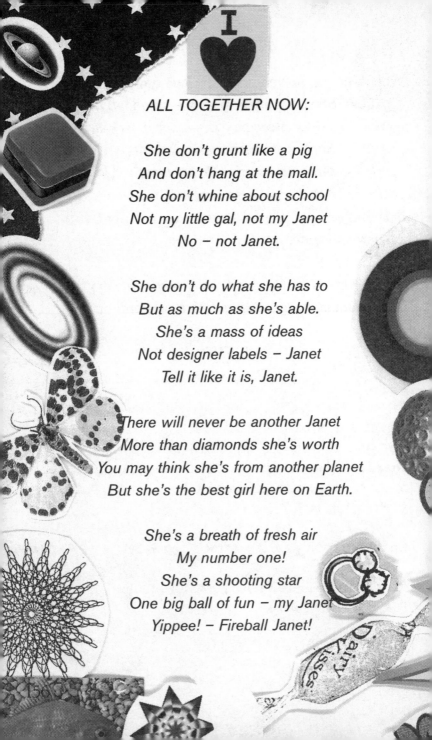

I ♥

ALL TOGETHER NOW:

She don't grunt like a pig
And don't hang at the mall.
She don't whine about school
Not my little gal, not my Janet
No – not Janet.

She don't do what she has to
But as much as she's able.
She's a mass of ideas
Not designer labels – Janet
Tell it like it is, Janet.

There will never be another Janet
More than diamonds she's worth
You may think she's from another planet
But she's the best girl here on Earth.

She's a breath of fresh air
My number one!
She's a shooting star
One big ball of fun – my Janet
Yippee! – Fireball Janet!

She's not waiting for the future
Or dwelling in the past
She's right here in the present
An enthusiast! – Smart Janet
Keep on smiling kid!

There will never be another Janet
More than diamonds she's worth
You may think she's from another planet
But she's the best girl here on Earth.

THE END

Me